D0099569

THIS BOOK IS A GIFT OF:
FRIENDS OF THE LAFAYETTE LIBRARY
CONTRA COSTA COUNTY LIBRARY

Animals That Ought To Be

I love my dogs. They lick my face,
fetch sticks, do tricks, catch balls, play chase.

I love the way my cats prefer
to curl up on my lap and purr.

I even like the little mouse
that squeaks around my grandpa's house.

Chicks and geese and pigs and sheep:
I count them all before I sleep.

But sometimes when I lie in bed
fantastic creatures fill my head.

Animals you never see.
Animals that ought to be.

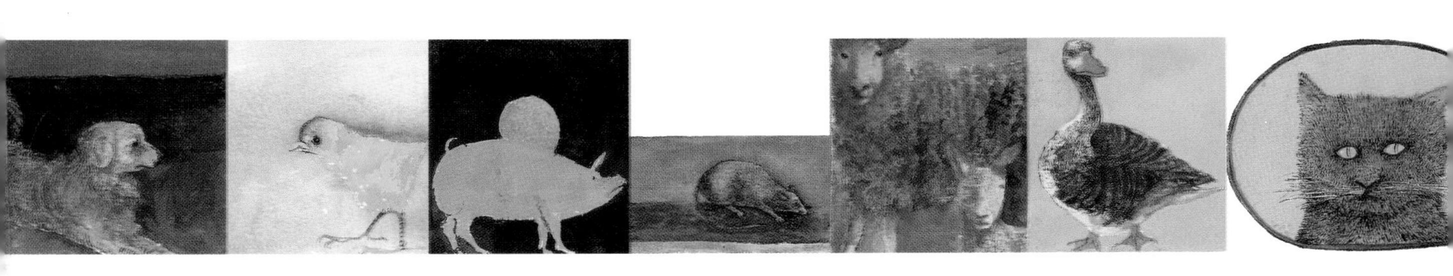

ANIMALS THAT OUGHT TO BE

POEMS ABOUT IMAGINARY PETS

by RICHARD MICHELSON
with paintings by
LEONARD BASKIN

SIMON & SCHUSTER BOOKS FOR YOUNG READERS

SIMON & SCHUSTER BOOKS FOR YOUNG READERS
An imprint of Simon & Schuster Children's Publishing Division
1230 Avenue of the Americas
New York, New York 10020

Book design by Anahid Hamparian
The text of this book is set in 14-point Cochin.
The illustrations are rendered in watercolor.
Printed and bound in the United States of America
First Edition

10 9 8 7 6 5 4 3 2 1

Library of Congress Cataloging-in-Publication Data

Michelson, Richard.
Animals that ought to be : poems about imaginary pets / by Richard Michelson ; paintings by Leonard Baskin.
p. cm.
Summary: A collection of short poems about all kinds of unusual animals, including the Backtalk Bat, the Roombroom, and the Channel Changer.
1. Imagination—Juvenile poetry. 2. Animals—Juvenile poetry.
3. Children's poetry, American. [1. Animals—Poetry. 2. Imagination—Poetry 3. American poetry.] I. Baskin, Lenoard, 1922– ill.
II. Title.
PS3563.I34A84 1996 811'.54—dc20 95-26262 CIP AC
ISBN 0-689-80635-3

For Marisa: May all your dreams come true

—R. M.

For Nicholas and for Ezekiel: To grow on

—L. B.

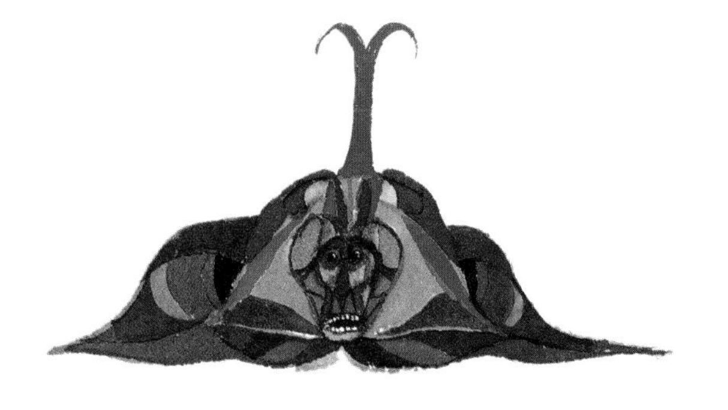

Contents

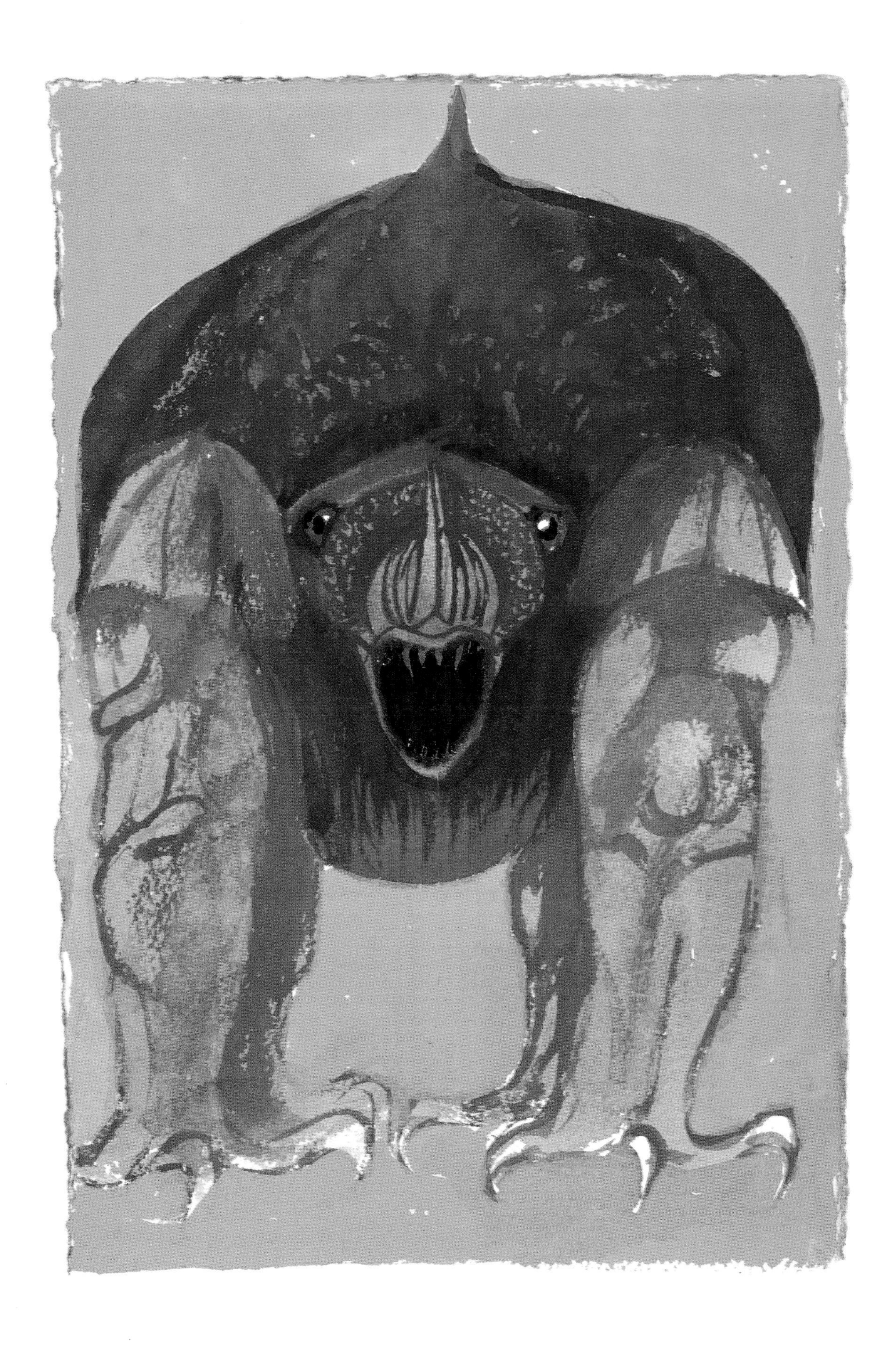

The Nightnoise Gladiator

When the radiator hisses,
when the hall stairs creak and moan,
when there's something downstairs ringing
but it's not the telephone;

When the back door lock is squeaking,
when you think you hear a knock,
when there's something upstairs ticking
and it's not Grandfather's clock;

When the refrigerator rattles,
when the window curtains swish,
when the bathroom sink *drip-drips, drip-drips,*
I close my eyes and wish

I had a Nightnoise Gladiator.
There is nothing he enjoys
more than eating till he's gobbled up
his enemy: Night Noise.

The Roombroom

When Mom tells me no more TV
until I clean my room,
I wait for a commercial,
then I whistle for Roombroom.

His whiskers are a whisk broom.
His nostrils are Dustbusters.
His backside is a vacuum.
His feathers, feather dusters.

It takes Roombroom one minute.
The problem is that then
it only takes me seconds
to mess things up again.

I'm-All-Ears

I always wondered what they said
after they tucked me into bed.

I used to tiptoe down the stairs
and hold my breath and say my prayers.

Well I don't do that anymore.
I'm nine now and much too mature.

Besides, I have an I'm-All-Ears.
I can't help what she overhears.

If someone's speaking very low
I'm-All-Ears' ears begin to grow.

They grow until she's overheard
and told me every single word.

She snacks on whispers. I can't stop her.
She's part gossip, part eavesdropper.

Talkback Bat

My brother is a big-mouth brat!
But when I tried to tell him that

my mother sent ME straight to bed.
"And don't talk back!" is what she said.

"HE started it. He's a world-famous
idiot and ignoramus,

"a nitwit, moron, maniac."
That's what I'd say if I talked back.

But my bat says the things I think:
"Numbskull! Dumbbell! Dunce! Rat fink!"

He shouts and screams, and all the while
I sit back blamelessly and smile.

Sweeteater

Most birds wake up early
and sing: *tweet tweet tweet tweet.*
Sweeteater sleeps till dinnertime,
then shouts: *Let's eat some sweets.*

Peanut butter cookies
and chocolate layer cake;
Most birds search for earthworms.
Sweeteater yells: *Let's bake.*

Most birds eat like . . . well birds.
They're grateful for a crumb.
Sweeteater serves us ice cream
and hums: *Yum yum yum yum.*

Tootsie Roll lollipops
and M & M's galore.
Most birds peck and nibble.
Sweeteater roars: *Eat more.*

Dad ordered us to diet:
"Too many sweets are bad!"
Sweeteater added sugar
then burped and ate my dad.

Nightmare Scarer

I have a Nightmare Scarer.
He hides beneath my bed.
He frightens off the nightmares
before they reach my head.

All spiders, snakes, and lizards,
all crawling things that creep,
know better than to enter
my mind while I'm asleep.

He's fierce as he is ugly.
He's mean without a doubt.
He'll chew up my worst nightmare
and then he'll spit it out.

There's just one tiny problem
that I did not foresee.
My Nightmare Scarer terrifies
and frightens even me.

The Backpack Snacker

She didn't get my cookie
or my french fries or Big Mac
but she swallowed up my homework.
The Backpack Snacker's back.

She chewed through half my fractions.
I'd have gotten an A+.
I double-checked my answers
twice, this morning on the bus.

She gobbled up my grammar
and I can't believe she ate
the last page of my book report,
but trust me, it was great.

She must have smelled my spelling words.
She swallowed the whole stack.
Don't blame me. I did my homework but . . .
The Backpack Snacker's back.

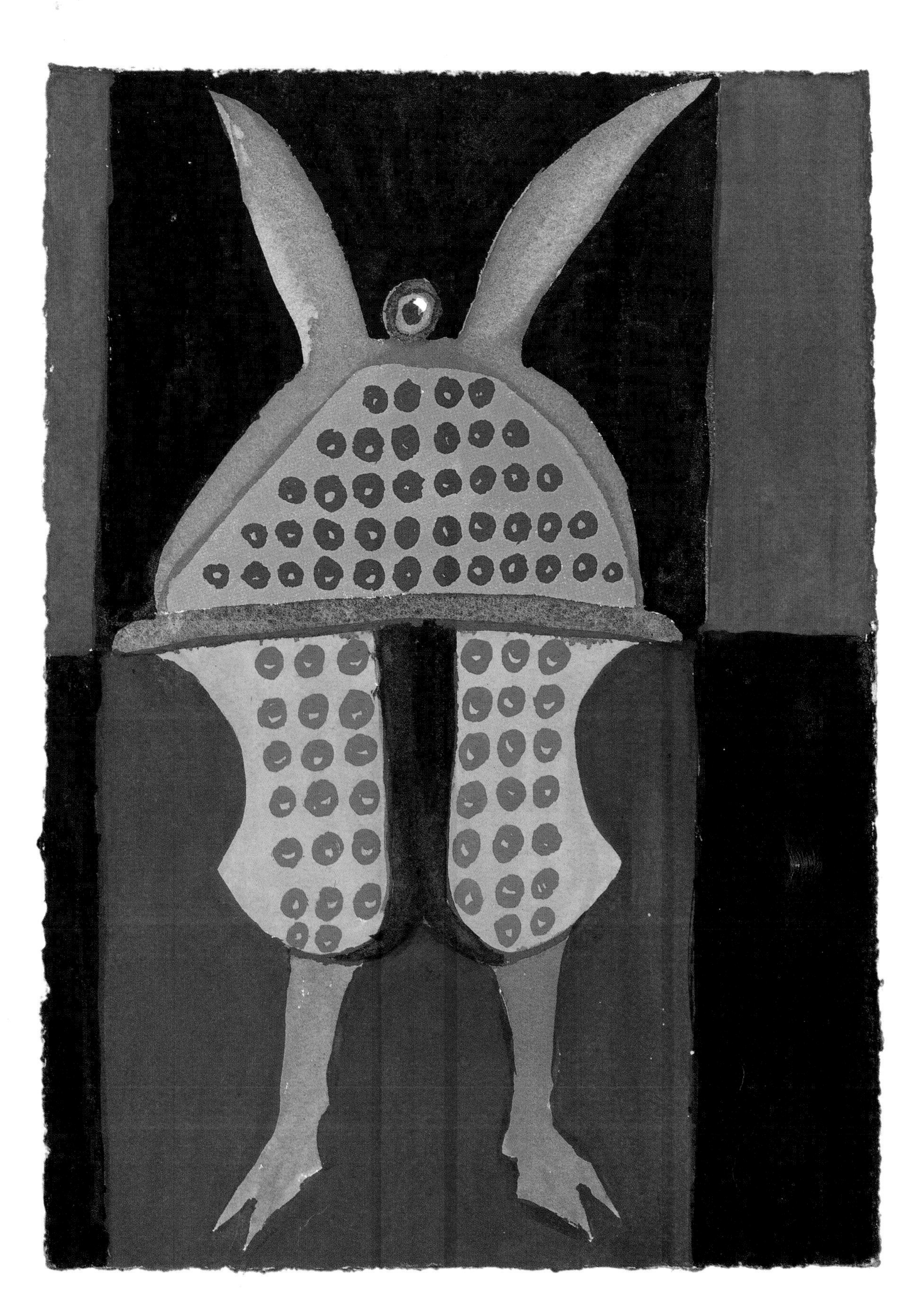

Channel Changer

We have a billion stations.
We have cable and of course
a satellite night hookup
with a backup power source.

We have a giant screen TV
with Dolby surround sound.
That darn remote control thing,
though, never can be found.

That's why a Channel Changer
is a pet beyond compare.
He surfs through the commercials
and he never needs repair.

His ears are each antennas.
His one eye is open wide.
I never have to walk him
since he hates to go outside.

He doesn't get much exercise
but anyone can tell he
loves to press each button
on his eighty-button belly.

Leftover Eater

They found a home for Boots.
They found a home for Rover.
But at the pound they had
one animal left over.

They said she loved leftovers,
but that she'd also eat
freshly buttered cow brains
and pigs with pickled feet.

Frog legs, fish eggs, liver,
and hot dogs when they're cold,
soup that smells like dirty socks
with three-week-old mold.

She ate up all our gross stuff.
The problem was that later,
she also ate my plate and . . .
the whole refrigerator.

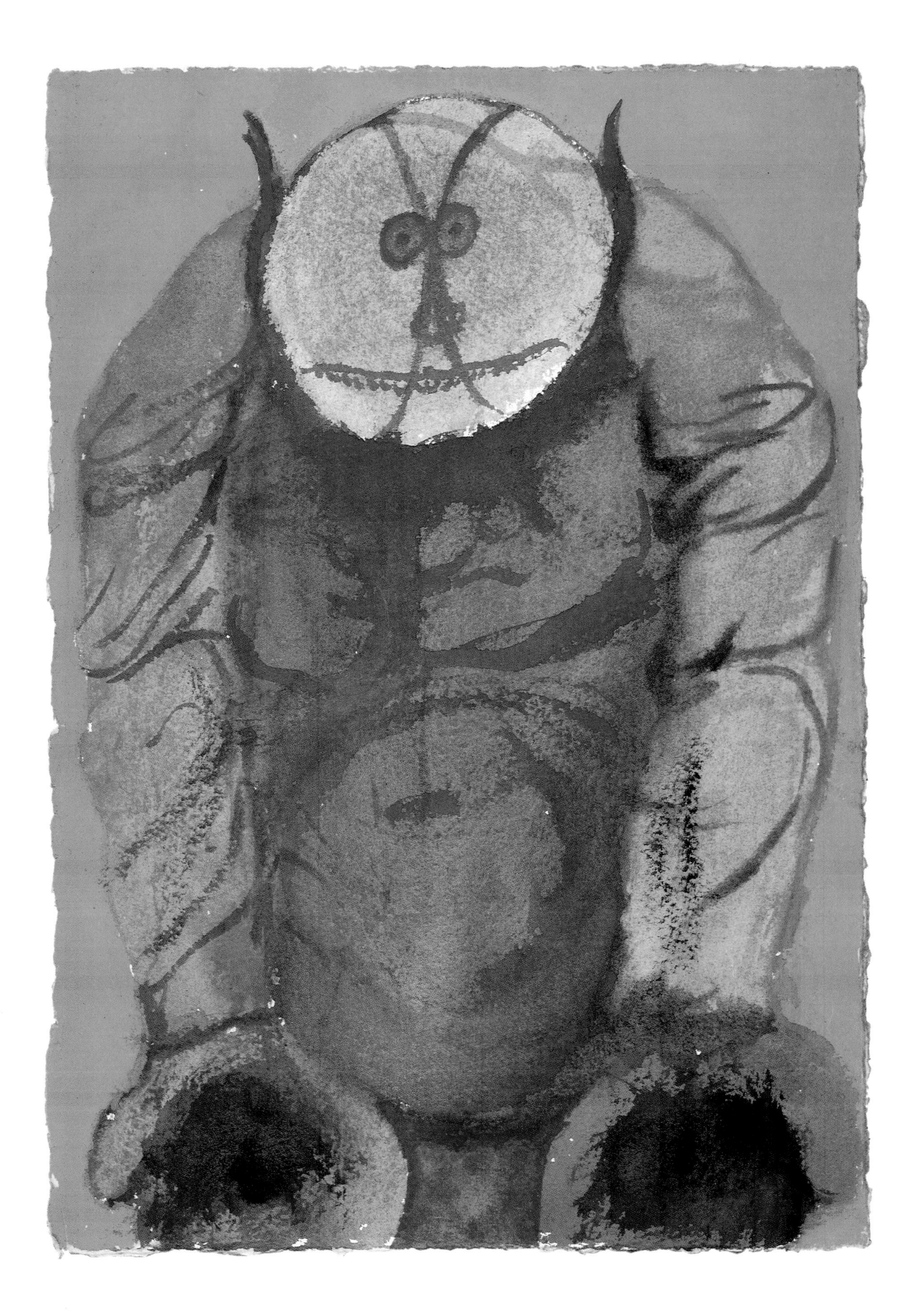

Buscatcher

"Hurry, hurry, hurry."
My mom makes such a fuss.
"You can't be late for school!"
she yells, "You'll miss the bus!"

But I'm still in my p.j.'s.
I don't know what to wear.
I haven't brushed my teeth yet
or combed a single hair.

Some kids would rush and worry.
Some kids would call it quits.
But their pets all have claws or paws.
My Buscatcher has mitts.

He'll chase the bus and catch it.
But this part is the best:
he'll hold it till I'm out of bed
and fed, brushed, combed, and dressed.

Nightlight Bird

I used to need a nightlight
when it was time for bed
until we got a red-eyed
Nightlight Bird instead.

I don't need any batteries
or bulbs or plugs or sockets.
I just keep Nightlight Bird seed
in my pajama pockets.

My bird won't scare a burglar.
She's slow and pigeon-toed,
but if she senses danger
Bird blinks and sends Morse Code.

But best of all, when Nightlight
starts her late-night stare
the shadows in my room run
away and disappear.

Yesnomaybe

When he was barely one year old, I took him to the vet
who said that Yesnomaybe was no ordinary pet.

"He may be just a baby but it's obvious to me,
he has two heads too many. I have counted. One, two, three.

"Maybe he'll grow to be a No, maybe he'll be a Yes,
maybe he'll be a Maybe. Here's my bill. Good luck. God bless."

Sometimes I can't decide myself—who I'll grow up to be.
Sometimes I think I'm happy and sometimes I disagree

and sometimes, just like Yesnomaybe, what I'd like to do
is hold my breath until my faces turn red, white, and blue.

Sometimes he smiles, sometimes not, and sometimes he will throw
a temper tantrum till I shout out "Yesnomaybe, NO!"

He's driving me half crazy but Mom says he's only two
and acting like all other Yesnomaybe babies do,

and though from year to year I'll hear "maybe" and "no," Mom guesses,
Yesnomaybe and I will both grow up to be big Yesses.

Animals That Ought To Be

I love to lie alone in bed
while wondrous creatures fill my head.

But still, there's nothing I've dreamed yet
that's better than a real live pet.

That's why I thank my lucky star
that animals are who they are.

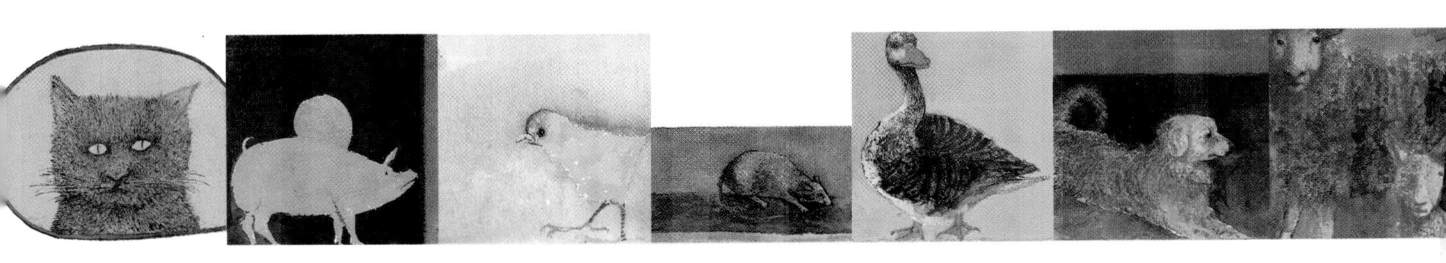